Detective Dylan and the Case of the Missing Mail

A Youth Sleuths Chapter Book Series

MJ Murray

Illustrated by
Amanda Letcher

The story, all names, characters, and incidents portrayed in this production are fictitious. No identification with actual persons (living or deceased), places, buildings, and products is intended or should be inferred.

Visit the author's website at www.mjmurraybooks.com

Illustrations: Amanda Letcher https://www.behance.net/amandaletcher

Paperback ISBN: 979-8-9888669-0-9

Hardcover ISBN: 979-8-9888669-1-6

Audiobook ISBN: 979-8-9888669-2-3

Ebook ISBN: 979-8-9888669-9-2

For Riley

Thank you for reminding me that a love for reading starts as soon as we're handed a book.

Contents

MAIL

Chapter 1

The Deluxe Detective Kit

It was the first week of summer break for 8-year-old Dylan, and he was bored. He sat on the sidewalk and waited for the mailman.

His sister, Emily the Tattle Tale, sat beside him because, well, she could. The worst part of summer was that Dylan had to spend each day with his sister. Morning and night. Yuck.

Their dog, Theodore, lay between them.

The warm sun felt nice after two rainy days in a row. Emily had a red popsicle that was melting faster than she could eat it.

Drip, drip, drip went the popsicle onto the ground.

Lick, lick, lick went Theodore's tongue onto the drips.

"Why do we have to wait out here, anyway?" Emily asked.

"We don't," said Dylan. "You can stay inside."

Emily made a face.

She asked, "Then how would I see what you're doing? Besides, mom says you have to be nice to me." Emily sat up. The popsicle waved close to Theodore's face. "I'm in kindergarten now."

"Not yet," said Dylan. He stuck his tongue out at Emily. "Not until school starts again. Until then, you are still a pre-school baby!"

"Take it back!" Emily said. She forgot about the popsicle in her hand.

Theodore watched the popsicle and squirmed. He couldn't sit still. First, his stubby tail moved back and forth. Then, he wriggled and twisted his body, not able to look away from the popsicle.

It looked so good! Finally, he gave it a quick lick.

No one saw. No one said, "*No, Theodore*".

Theodore leaned forward as slowly as he could. Two more big licks and the popsicle was gone. Now, only the stick was left. He put his head between his paws to look like he was asleep.

Dylan didn't want Emily to tattle. She was good at that. He said, "Fine, I take it back. And I told you. I'm waiting for the mail."

"But why?" asked Emily.

"For the last time, my detective kit will be here today," Dylan said.

It wasn't just any detective kit.

This was *the* deluxe detective kit sold by his favorite show, Youth Sleuths! Dylan had watched every episode on his tablet. He had watched some of them twice.

In every episode, the detectives used clues to solve a crime that no one else could solve. Dylan wanted to be just like them.

"Can I play too?" asked Emily.

"Maybe," said Dylan. He didn't want to share. He also didn't want Emily to have a fit.

Just then, Dylan heard a truck. He looked and saw the mail truck heading his way. It was here!

The mailman, Mr. Ben, stopped in front of the mailbox. Dylan jumped up to see what Mr. Ben was putting in the mailbox. It looked like it was only letters.

Dylan frowned. "Hi, Mr. Ben. Do you have anything else for us?"

"Yes, but it's too big for the mailbox," said Mr. Ben with a grin. He lifted a box from the truck. It was large and orange and said YOUTH SLEUTHS in big letters across the top.

"That's for me!" said Dylan. He grabbed the box and was so happy he forgot to say thank you. He ran to the house before he realized he had also forgotten Theodore and Emily.

He opened the front door and called, "Emily! Theodore! Come inside now!" before he ran inside.

This was the greatest day ever.

Chapter 2

Mailbox Mystery

Dylan ripped open the box and looked inside. On top was a sheet of paper.

To: All Youth Sleuths Fans

Congratulations on your very own Youth Sleuths deluxe detective kit! Inside this box, you will find all the items you need to be an official Youth Sleuths detective. Use them to collect your own clues.

Contents:
1 magnifying glass
1 pair of binoculars
1 fingerprint collection kit
2 clue containers

1 whistle

1 Youth Sleuths note-pad

1 Youth Sleuths pen

1 Youth Sleuths ID badge with slot for your picture!

Theodore sniffed the box. It did not smell like food, so he ducked under the table to rest.

"What's this?" asked Emily. She picked up the notepad.

"Put that down," said Dylan. He grabbed the notepad and checked it for dirt. "Mom said you have to respect my toys. That means you need to ask before using my toys and not mess with them or break them either!"

Emily stuck out her tongue at Dylan. She backed away from the box.

"Will you share with me?" she asked.

He shook his head. "This kit cost 8 weeks of allowance. It means a lot to me," said Dylan.

Before Emily could act upset, Dylan added, "But

you can hang out with me and I can give you some paper to use, too."

Dylan opened the ID badge and carefully wrote his name inside it. Then he glued his school picture next to his name. Once it dried, he pinned it to the front of his shirt.

They returned to the front yard. Their neighbor was looking in her mailbox.

"Hello, Mrs. Lane," said Dylan.

She smiled at Dylan and Emily. "Hello, my dears. Have you seen my mail? I just got back from a trip and my mailbox is empty."

"No," said Emily. She held her paper in one hand. Her other hand held Theodore's collar. Theodore tugged on it, trying to reach Mrs. Lane. Nothing made him happier than food and belly rubs.

"Me neither," said Dylan.

Then, he had an idea! He pulled his Youth Sleuths notepad and pen out of his pocket.

"Mrs. Lane," said Dylan. "Can we help you find it? I'm a detective now."

He stood up tall to show how grown he looked and pointed at his badge.

Mrs. Lane smiled at Dylan.

"That would be great," said Mrs. Lane. "In fact, I'll give you a $10 reward if you can locate it."

$10? That was two weeks' worth of allowance!

"Sure!" said Dylan with a big grin. He got his pen ready to take notes.

"What mail do you know is missing?" he asked.

"A coupon book. Oh, and a check I need to deposit at the bank," said Mrs. Lane. "But most importantly, there were pictures of my grandkids. I must get those back!"

"We're on it," Dylan said. He waved goodbye to Mrs. Lane as she headed back into her house.

Chapter 3

I Like Cookies

Dylan grabbed his fingerprint kit and his whistle from inside the house.

"In Youth Sleuths, they always start by asking people if they saw anything," Dylan said.

Emily had never watched the show, but she nodded anyway. This was her chance to play with Dylan! She planned to agree with anything he said today.

"Who should we ask first?" she asked.

"Let's start with Mr. Bloom," said Dylan.

Dylan carried his detective kit and headed to the blue house across the street. Emily and Theodore followed.

He knocked once. There was no answer.

Not wanting to give up, Dylan knocked a second time. Then he knocked again.

Mr. Bloom opened the door after the third knock.

He looked like he had been asleep, but the yellow ducks on his pajamas were wide awake. The glasses on his face were crooked. There was very little hair on his head. The hairs he did have were sticking up and messy.

"Yes?" Mr. Bloom asked. He looked at Emily and frowned. "I don't want to buy any cookies."

"Cookies?" asked Emily. "I like cookies."

Theodore's ears moved in excitement. He liked cookies too.

They both leaned to look around Mr. Bloom. They didn't see any cookies inside his house.

"No, Mr. Bloom. We're not here to sell anything," said Dylan. "We are here to tell you Mrs. Lane has missing mail."

"And to ask you if you saw anything," Emily said.

Dylan pulled out his detective ID and held up it to Mr. Bloom.

"Saw anything?" asked Mr. Bloom. "What would I have seen?"

Emily drew on her paper as Mr. Bloom talked. Dylan saw a stick figure of a man with three single hairs sticking up on top of his head.

Theodore rolled onto his back and hoped his new friend would pet him.

Dylan pointed across the street. "Did you see anyone open Mrs. Lane's mailbox?" he asked.

Mr. Bloom scratched his chin. "I don't think so," he said.

Dylan pulled out his fingerprint kit. He asked, "Do you mind if I get your fingerprint so I can see if it matches fingerprints on the mailbox?"

"I do mind!" said Mr. Bloom. "Why would I go in her mailbox without her asking me to?"

"We're just trying to help Mrs. Lane," said Emily with a grin.

"Kids, I am exhausted! I have not slept well the past few days. I am so tired I can barely keep my eyes open or stand up. I think it is time for you to ask someone else now," he said.

"Ok. Thank you for your help," said Dylan. "If you remember anything, please come tell me."

Emily had now drawn little 'z' shapes on her paper.

Theodore waited on his back for his new friend to see him.

Mr. Bloom shut the door, but then opened it again.

"There is one thing that I don't understand," he said. "Usually Mrs. Lane asks me to watch her house . She has me collect her mail when she goes out of town. This time, she didn't ask me. I don't know why."

Chapter 4

Cats and Dogs

Dylan and Emily walked to the house next door. Theodore sniffed the grass as he followed behind them.

"What if Mr. Bloom took the mail?" Emily asked.

"He said he hadn't seen it," Dylan said.

"That doesn't mean he didn't take it," said Emily stubbornly.

"But why would he take it?" Dylan asked. "It doesn't make sense."

Emily frowned.

They were on the porch when the garage door opened. A blue van pulled out and honked.

BEEP. BEEP.

The back seats were filled with kids. The window rolled down and a lady with big curly hair said,

"Dylan! Emily! Hi! No time to talk. Judy is late for swim practice! See you later!"

"Thanks, Mrs. Maddle," said Dylan, but she was already driving away.

Dylan used his binoculars to watch her drive down the street. One kid in the van had her face pressed against the window. Around her was a pile of pool toys.

Dylan could see a blue pool noodle and a yellow beach bag with a smiley face on it. He even saw a giant striped ball that looked like one Theodore had popped last week!

"Maybe we need to move on to the next house," said Emily.

Dylan put his detective kit down.

"Maybe not," he said. "Maybe I can get a fingerprint off of the door."

He opened the kit and looked at the fingerprint tape. He didn't know what to do. Emily didn't need to know that.

He stuck the tape on the door and then pulled it off. He was holding it up to the light when Theodore made him jump.

BARK.

BARK BARK.

Dylan turned to see Theodore run across the grass toward an orange cat. No one was holding Theodore's leash and no one could stop him!

The cat stretched and moved its tail from side to side. It acted like it *wanted* Theodore to see it.

Right before Theodore reached it, the cat ran down the sidewalk.

Dylan shouted, "Theodore, stop!", but Theodore ignored him. Theodore acted like he didn't hear Dylan. He made sure he didn't look back at Emily and Dylan. Then Theodore ran after the cat!

"Oh no!" cried Emily. "What if he gets lost?"

"We need to follow him," said Dylan. He dropped everything and ran.

Dylan and Emily ran after Theodore. Theodore

ran after the cat. The cat ran, enjoying the game it had started.

The cat jumped over a basketball and dove under a car. It even ran through two girls jumping rope! It passed three more houses before Dylan caught up. Dylan grabbed Theodore's leash and pulled him to a stop.

Theodore cried. He pulled on the leash. He really wanted that cat!

The cat jumped on a fence and licked its paws. It looked like it was smiling. Theodore couldn't reach it now.

"Whoa," said Emily. "This is the very end of our street. What would have happened if Theodore had crossed?"

Dylan gripped the leash tightly with his hand. "We got lucky," he said.

He looked down and remembered he had forgotten his detective kit back at Mrs. Maddle's house. "Hurry! We need to go back and get our notes!"

Chapter 5

Snack in the Garden

Dylan and Emily gathered their detective items and crossed the street.

Theodore followed, stubby tail between his legs. He knew he shouldn't have chased the cat.

Dylan walked into the yard next door to Mrs. Lane's house. "Maybe Miss Maria saw something," he said.

Miss Maria was in her front yard planting flowers.

"Hi, Miss Maria," said Emily.

Miss Maria dusted the dirt off her hands. "Hi, Emily. Hello, Dylan. How's your day going?"

"Great," said Dylan. "I'm a detective now!"

"Oh my!" said Miss Maria. "What about you, Emily? Are you a detective, too?"

Emily glared at Dylan. “I’m just his helper.”

Miss Maria laughed. “Well, I was about to have some lemonade. Would the detective and his *helpful* helper like to join me?”

“We sure would!” said Dylan.

Miss Maria went into the house. She came back with a large tray. It was piled high with food.

They had never seen such a feast! On the tray was a pitcher of lemonade, three glasses, a pile of grapes, a chunk of cheese, and a tower of crackers. There was also a bowl with two kinds of cookies! Miss Maria even had a dog treat shaped like a bone for Theodore.

They ate until they were all very full.

Theodore fell asleep on the grass. He was having a big dream. His legs twitched slightly, and he made quiet growling noises.

"Those were the best cookies ever," said Emily.

She licked her fingers and wiped them on her shirt. There was still chocolate on her face.

"They sure were!" said Dylan.

"Did you children come over just to say hello?" asked Miss Maria.

"Oh, I almost forget!" said Dylan. "I'm—"

He stopped talking as Emily gave him three sharp pokes.

He rolled his eyes and said, "*We* are helping Mrs. Lane track down her missing mail. Have you seen anything?"

"Hmm." Miss Maria thought for a few seconds. "You know, I saw something yesterday."

"You did?" asked Emily. She jumped up and down.

"What did you see?" shouted Dylan.

The noise woke Theodore. He looked around and yawned. He stretched and rested one paw on Miss Maria. She smiled and scratched his belly.

"Well, kids. I'm not sure I'll be much help," she said. "I was working in the garden but didn't have my glasses on. I saw movement over by Mrs. Lane's mailbox but didn't see anything else."

Dylan was taking notes as fast as he could! He knew just what the Youth Sleuths would do.

"That's great," he said. "Now, let's try a trick to help you. Close your eyes and think about that day."

Miss Maria closed her eyes. She kept petting Theodore. He was now on his back and stretched across her lap. He looked like a big, furry baby.

"Can you remember what the weather was like?" Dylan asked.

"Yes, it rained. The dirt was soft and muddy," said Miss Maria.

"Great! Now, did you smell anything?" asked Dylan.

"Yes! It smelled like the lavender I planted," Miss Maria said.

Dylan grinned and said, "Ok. You felt the soft dirt, and you smelled the lavender. Did you hear anything?"

Miss Maria gasped and her eyes flew open! "I did! I did! I heard the mailbox open. It was rusty and loud. I turned to look and saw someone carrying something bright yellow!"

It was Emily's turn to gasp. She looked at her brother. Maybe Dylan was a real detective, after all.

Chapter 6

Guard Dog

Dylan, Emily, and Theodore ran back to their house. They couldn't believe their luck. This was their first real clue!

Emily grabbed two cups of water and sat next to Dylan at the kitchen table. Dylan spread out his notes, putting the paper with the word "yellow" on top.

Emily put her drawing of Mr. Bloom on the table, too.

Dylan pushed it aside. "This table is for clues," he said.

Emily shrugged. She pushed the paper back. "Maybe Mr. Bloom gave us a clue, too. He *said* Mrs. Lane asks him for help sometimes," she said.

Dylan didn't like Emily's suggestion. Her idea

didn't make sense. Mr. Bloom didn't give them their first clue. He didn't take the mail either. Dylan was sure that the yellow object Miss Maria saw was their first clue.

He looked at the notes on the table and ignored Emily.

"Someone took Mrs. Bloom's mail. What if they do it again? What if they take our mail?" he asked.

"Oh no! We gotta stop them," said Emily.

Dylan picked his notes back up. "Let's walk Theodore around the block as a guard dog. Just until we figure out who took the mail."

Emily laughed.

"Theodore isn't a guard dog," she said.

Theodore looked at Emily and Dylan. They were both saying his name, but he wasn't sure what they wanted. He licked each of their faces.

No, licking wasn't what they wanted.

He picked up his favorite toy ball and carried it to Emily. She didn't throw it.

No, they didn't want to play with the ball.

Theodore sniffed Emily's hands. They smelled like cookies. She waved him away.

He looked for food crumbs, anyway. He smelled the tabletop, the chair, and his own bottom before lying down at their feet.

Dylan grabbed the leash and whistled at Theodore. "Come on, boy," Dylan said.

Dylan and Emily walked Theodore across the front yard and down the sidewalk. They circled the block three times, looking for a person with a yellow object.

"What does a person who steals mail look like?" asked Emily.

Dylan didn't know. "Well, they look like a bad guy," he said.

"What does a bad guy look like?" Emily asked.

"Suspicious," Dylan said. That was a word that the Youth Sleuths used. Dylan didn't know what the word actually meant, but it sounded like something a detective would say.

Emily stopped and frowned. "What is supsitious," she asked.

Dylan rolled his eyes at Emily and said, "I don't have time to teach you everything!".

Emily sat on the sidewalk. She wrapped her arms around her legs. She looked like she might cry.

Dylan felt bad.

"I'm sorry," he said. "I don't know what suspicious means, either. It's just a word I heard from Youth Sleuths."

Emily sniffled. "It's ok," she said. "I have an idea of how we can find the missing mail."

"Yeah?" Dylan asked.

"Well, I was thinking we could talk to the kids who live on our block. We can ask them what they saw. Grownups don't always look around. But kids do," she said.

"Sure, let's try it," said Dylan. He was very glad Emily hadn't cried.

Chapter 7

Calling All Kids

Dylan and Emily gathered the kids from their street.

José and Jack stopped playing kickball. Jack's little brother, Scotty, came too. Scotty always wore a big yellow poncho, even when it was sunny.

Alice, Jennifer, and Riley stopped their tea party.

Everyone except Mrs. Maddle's kids showed up. They were still at swim practice.

Finally, the kids circled around Theodore. Theodore ran from kid to kid. Each kid laughed as Theodore licked their hands and faces.

"All right, everyone," said Dylan.

No one looked at him.

Dylan tried again, louder this time. "Ahem!"

No. That didn't work either. Dylan needed to get their attention. He wanted the kids to see him. They needed to hear what he had to say. This was a big deal!

Dylan grabbed his whistle. He blew it once. Twice. Three times!

The sound was very loud. Now everyone was looking at him. Everyone was also covering their ears. Even Theodore was sitting still. His tail wagged softly.

Dylan grinned and made sure his badge was straight.

"Hi, everyone," said Dylan.

Dylan had everyone's attention. But now he wasn't sure what to say.

"Yeah?" asked José.

Dylan's cheeks were red. "Um," he said.

Emily jumped up. "We need your help!"

Everyone turned to look at Emily.

"With what?" asked Riley.

"Mrs. Lane's mail is missing," said Emily. "And we're helping her."

Dylan was glad that Emily helped him. He was ready to take over now.

"We think the mail was taken yesterday. By someone wearing yellow," said Dylan.

"Wait," said Emily. "I thought Miss Maria saw someone *holding* something yellow?"

Dylan frowned. He wasn't sure. "Well, Miss Maria saw *something* yellow when it happened."

"What if it was Scotty?" asked Alice. Everyone laughed.

"No, I mean it," she said. "Look at him. He's wearing a yellow poncho."

"Don't be silly," said Jack.

Everyone looked at Scotty. Scotty was really young. He grinned and drooled while petting Theodore.

"I'm not sure Scotty can reach the mailbox," said Dylan. "He probably didn't take the mail."

"I think the Maddle family has a yellow beach bag. I tripped on it the other day when they left it on the sidewalk," said Riley. "Oh! Dylan? Doesn't your mom have a yellow umbrella?"

Dylan frowned. Why would either of them want Mrs. Lane's mail?

Jack lowered his voice. "What if it was the Benny brothers?" he asked.

Emily gasped.

"Who are the Benny brothers?" Jennifer asked. She was new to the street. She hadn't whispered her question. Alice made a hushing noise.

Everyone else looked to check if the Benny brothers had heard.

Jack whispered, "The Benny brothers are the twins who live on the next block. They are mean fourth graders. Everyone has been pranked by them!"

Emily added, "They set off firecrackers. It scares our dog."

"They popped my tube at the pool," said Riley.

Dylan hoped the Benny brothers hadn't taken the mail. He wasn't ready for that kind of action.

"They are the worst!" said Jack.

"Did anyone see the Benny brothers with the mail?" asked Dylan.

Everyone shook their heads.

"Ok, then let's leave them alone," said Dylan.

Dylan liked making these decisions. He felt like a real detective!

Chapter 8

Monster Tracks

Dylan and Emily walked back to Mrs. Lane's house. Emily struggled with Theodore's leash.

Theodore wanted to stay with the other kids.

"What do we do now?" asked Emily.

"I think we need to investigate some more," said Dylan. "Let's start with what we've done so far."

"Well," Emily said. "We've talked to the people around us."

"And we've collected clues," added Dylan. "Do we have enough clues to find out the truth?"

Emily said, "Hmm. We think the mail was taken yesterday after it rained."

"We think the person was wearing or carrying something yellow," said Dylan.

Emily shrugged. She said, "And Mr. Bloom usually watches Mrs. Lane's house. But not this time."

They both thought quietly.

"We know when and where it happened. We don't know who, though. I'm not sure we have enough clues," Dylan said.

Dylan had a sudden idea!

It was so simple, he didn't know why he hadn't thought of it before.

Dylan grabbed the magnifying glass out of his detective kit. He ran to Mrs. Lane's mailbox.

"Emily, come here!" he called.

Emily ran over.

"What is it?" she asked.

"Look!" Dylan said. He pointed at the ground under the mailbox.

Emily leaned down.

The ground was still muddy from the rain. There wasn't any grass.

In the mud, there were two triangle shaped marks. Next to each triangle was a tiny circle.

It looked like someone had stuck a pencil tip into the mud.

"What is this?" Dylan asked.

Emily looked around. She was suddenly scared. "Are those monster tracks?"

"I don't think so," said Dylan.

"Well, those are *not* people tracks," said Emily.

"I'm not sure what those are," said Dylan.

He leaned down to look closer.

Emily used a crayon to draw the marks they saw. The triangles and circles didn't take up very much space on the page.

Not sure what else to do, she added a silly-looking monster on the top of the page. On top of his stick body was a large head with five eyes. She drew hearts where his teeth should be. His triangle shaped feet were big. Last, she gave him long pink fur.

Theodore sniffed the mud around the marks. He

pushed his nose into the mud, making a mess. Something smelled good!

"Theodore, no digging," said Dylan.

Theodore did not stop.

Normally, Theodore was good at doing what he was asked. Today, he was good at ignoring Dylan. He used one paw to scratch the dirt. Something was sticking out of the mud. It was shiny.

Emily saw it too.

"Look," Emily said.

Dylan let Theodore keep digging.

Soon, they could see a small toy sticking out of the mud.

"Good boy," said Dylan.

Dylan pulled the toy out of the mud and ran to the house to wash it off.

It was a tiny blue boat.

"Whoa," said Emily. "That is definitely a clue too. I bet the person who took the mail dropped it!"

"This boat is a little kid toy. There's no way the Benny brothers would have dropped it," said Dylan.

"Neither would Mr. Bloom," added Emily. "Who *would* have a toy boat?"

"I'm not sure," said Dylan. "Let's go tell Mrs. Lane about this."

Chapter 9

A Little Blue Boat

"Mrs. Lane," Dylan called as he knocked on her door.

It seemed to take hours for her to come outside.

Theodore sniffed every board on the porch while they waited.

They sat on the porch swing and told Mrs. Lane about their detective work.

When they finished, Dylan said, "We're sorry that we didn't find your mail."

"It's fine," said Mrs. Lane. "I can have my family send more pictures. Thank you for trying to find the mail."

"Just keep your eye out for people in yellow or monsters with triangle feet," said Emily.

"Hmm," said Mrs. Lane. "I'd prefer to see a person and not a monster. But if I had a choice, I think I'd just prefer to have my mail back."

Just then, Mrs. Maddle's van parked across the street. Kids climbed out of it. Pool toys fell out. Toys rolled across the driveway. Mrs. Maddle's arms were full as she crossed her yard. She dropped a stack of towels on the porch.

The kids ran around the yard. All were laughing and screaming.

One girl was wearing a pair of her mom's shoes. They were high heels and way too big. She had used thick tape to keep them from falling off her feet.

"I'll be right back," Dylan said.

Dylan crossed the street. Maybe Mrs. Maddle would have some information about the mystery. Maybe he could solve the crime after all.

"Oh, hello Dylan! Would you mind helping me?" Mrs. Maddle asked.

She piled pool toys into his arms and grabbed a big bag for herself. Dylan followed her.

Mrs. Maddle was carrying a big beach bag. The faded smiley face on it stared at him.

Wait!

This beach bag was yellow!

Just then, a little boy started crying.

"Dylan, do you mind bringing these toys to Henry?" Mrs. Maddle asked.

Dylan nodded. He was thinking about the yellow bag.

Mrs. Maddle pulled out a handful of small toy boats out of the bag.

Dylan held them and walked toward Henry.

Henry was still crying. Theodore crossed the street and licked Henry's feet.

Wait!

The toy boats looked familiar. Dylan pulled the clue from the mailbox out of his pocket. The clue boat and toy boats were the same!

He saw Mrs. Maddle cross the street to Mrs. Lane's house. She carried the bag.

"Hello, Mrs. Lane," said Mrs. Maddle.

Dylan ran across the street.

"Mrs. Lane!" he shouted. "I think I solved the crime."

"What crime?" asked Mrs. Maddle.

"Someone took Mrs. Lane's mail," said Emily.

"And I know who!" said Dylan.

"Oh, that was me!" said Mrs. Maddle.

Dylan frowned. He had just solved the clues. *He* wanted to tell Mrs. Lane that Mrs. Maddle took the mail.

She put down the beach bag and pulled out a stack of letters.

"Your mailbox was full yesterday," Mrs. Maddle said. "It was raining and I know your mailbox leaks. I didn't want your mail to get wet."

"Oh, thank you," said Mrs. Lane. She was smiling.

"I think I forgot to leave a note," said Mrs. Maddle.

"That's all right," said Mrs. Lane. "I forgot to ask someone to get my mail while I was gone. Thank you for keeping it dry!"

Dylan held up the toy boat.

"You dropped this at the mailbox," he said.

"Wait," said Emily. "If you took the mail, where did the monster tracks come from?"

"Monster tracks?" asked Mrs. Maddle.

Dylan grinned. He'd figured that part of the mystery out, too! He rushed forward to explain.

"Let me show you," said Dylan.

He walked over to the mailbox and pointed to the mud.

Mrs. Maddle frowned.

Then her eyes lit up. "I know!" she said.

"I do, too!" said Dylan. He pointed across the street at one of the Maddle children.

Mrs. Maddle waved. "Mary, come over here please."

The girl wearing the oversized shoes walked slowly across the street.

"Mary, lift one of your shoes up," Dylan said.

Mary lifted her shoe. The front part was a triangle. On the back was a skinny part.

Emily and Dylan laughed. The monster tracks weren't from a monster after all. They were from a little girl with too-big shoes.

Chapter 10

Bedtime

Dylan brushed his teeth and climbed into bed.

Soon, he heard Emily walk through the bathroom they shared.

She carried a pillow and a blanket.

Theodore followed behind her.

"Can I sleep in your room?" she asked.

"Sure," said Dylan.

Emily slept in his room most nights.

She made herself comfortable on the floor. Emily set up her pillow and blanket. Dylan helped her carry stuffed animals into his room. Emily placed them around her pillow in a line. The animals stretched almost all the way to the door.

Dylan covered Emily with her blanket. Theodore crawled under the blanket as well. Only his nose stuck out.

Within minutes, Theodore was snoring.

"I had a lot of fun today," Emily said.

"Me too," said Dylan. "Thanks for your help."

"I can't believe Mrs. Bloom gave you the $10 reward even though you didn't *completely* solve the crime," said Emily.

"Me neither!" said Dylan. He grinned and thought about what he would do with the reward. Maybe he would share it with Emily.

"Next time you have a detective case, can I help too?" Emily asked.

"I think I'd like that," said Dylan. And that was the truth!

"Can I be a detective, too?" Emily asked.

"Not yet. But you can be my assistant," Dylan said.

Emily grinned.

"I can't wait!" said Emily.

It was exciting to think about what they would solve next.

Dylan and Emily each had wonderful dreams that night. Both dreamed they were real detectives. Not even the Benny brothers scared them.

Theodore also dreamed. In his dreams, he had a never-ending bowl of food.

Author's Note

If you enjoyed this book and would like to help other people find it too, please consider asking your parent/guardian to post a brief review on the platform you purchased your book from. This book is self-published and every single review is appreciated!

The author has two dogs at home and reads every review out loud to them. The dogs especially enjoy reviews that mention Theodore.

Book #2 Coming Spring 2024!

Detective Dylan and the Hunt for Home Plate

Meet the Characters

Want to learn more about Dylan, Emily, and Theodore? Look no further for a behind-the-scenes look at the characters with the author!

Question: Is this book part of a series?
Author: That is the plan! It turns out, Dylan *really* enjoyed solving the mail mystery in this book. Which is probably a good thing because Dylan and Emily have sort of turned into mystery magnets now. They don't know it yet, but they are about to start attracting unsolved mysteries everywhere they go!

Question: Is Emily really a tattletale?
Author: Dear readers, I'll let you decide that for yourself. Do you know what an opinion is? An

opinion is what someone thinks. Maybe it is true. Maybe it isn't.

Confused? Let me help.
A fact is something that is true.
Here is a fact: *Theodore is a dog.*

Here is the author's opinion: *Theodore is the most adorable dog in the entire world.*

So, is Emily a tattletale? Dylan's opinion is that she is a tattletale. Emily's opinion is that she isn't a tattletale. After reading Book #1, what is **your** opinion?

Question: When is Theodore's birthday?
Author: Theodore isn't sure. Dylan and Emily adopted him from a shelter. Theodore loves his new family so much, he thinks every day is his birthday!

Question: Is Youth Sleuths a real show?
Author: No, but maybe it could be! Can you imagine banding together with your classmates and solving crimes with Dylan, Emily, and Theodore? No piece of homework or spare sock would ever go missing again!

ELA and Math Resources

Educators: use the QR code below or visit the author's website at www.mjmurraybooks.com for information on ELA/Math resources available for this book.

Classroom Prompts

Not ready to download the ELA/Math resources? Tailor the example prompts below for use in the classroom.

This book includes Tier 2 high frequency words of Common Core Academic Vocabulary for grades K and 1.

Chapter #1

Tier 2 word: Squirm

Prompt: In the text, Theodore squirms because he wants the popsicle. Who here has a pet that would act the same way? What are some things that would make people squirm? What about a mosquito bite you are trying not to scratch?

Chapter #2

Tier 2 word: Respect

Prompt: In the text, Dylan asks Emily to respect his toys. What are some ways we can treat classroom items with respect?

Chapter #3

Tier 2 word: Exhausted

Prompt: In the text, Mr. Bloom tells Dylan that he is exhausted because he hasn't gotten enough sleep. Do you think it is easier or harder to learn when we are exhausted?

Chapter #4

Tier 2 word: Ignore

Prompt: In the text, Theodore ignores Dylan and chases the cat. We know that Theodore *did* hear

Dylan. Why do you think Theodore ignored Dylan and chased the cat anyway?

Chapter #5

Tier 2 word: Feast

Prompt: In the text, Miss Maria brings out a large tray of food for Dylan, Emily, and Theodore. There was so much food, it was a feast! If our classroom had a feast, what food would you bring to it?

Chapter #6

Tier 2 word: Suggestion

Prompt: In the text, Emily has a suggestion for Dylan. She thinks Mr. Bloom gave them a clue. Why do you think Dylan didn't agree with her suggestion? If you were Dylan, do you think you'd listen to Emily's suggestions?

Chapter #7

Tier 2 word: Attention

Prompt: In the text, Dylan uses a whistle to get the other kids' attention. What are some things I do as your teacher to get the attention of the class?

Chapter #8

Tier 2 word: Investigate

Prompt: In the text, Dylan and Emily discuss ways to investigate the mail mystery. They asked questions and collected clues. If our playground balls/toys disappeared, what things could our class do to investigate?

Chapter #9

Tier 2 word: Prefer

Prompt: In the text, Mrs. Bloom says she'd prefer to see a person over a monster. If she had a choice, she'd prefer to get her mail back. When we prefer something, we'd rather have it than the other thing. If given the choice, would you prefer to have a longer recess or no homework for the day?

Chapter #10

Tier 2 word: Comfortable

Prompt: In the text, Emily uses blankets and stuffed animals to make herself comfortable for bedtime. If you could bring anything to the classroom to make yourself comfortable for story time, what would you bring?

Made in the USA
Las Vegas, NV
24 January 2024